The

Knowing

- JB STRATON'S STORY -

A Bulwark Anthology
Volume 1

BRIT LUNDEN

Illustrations by RL Jackson
No part of this publication may be reproduced, transmitted, stored, etc. Without the written permission of the author.

DEDICATION

For David, forever.

A soul mate is not found. A soul mate is recognized.
– Vironika Tugaleva

CONTENTS

1

SCRIMMAGE

BULWARK, GEORGIA – PRESENT DAY

JB closed the door gently, glad to have the place to himself again. Sheriff Clay Finnes had taken the injured couple to the hospital.

The only sound in the cabin was the creak of the wooden floors settling and the tick of the antique regulator clock that hung on the wall.

It was an old clock and had never worked very well. JB smiled, thinking Ellie would be pleased to see the ornate second hand traveling around the parchment-colored face and the great brass pendulum swinging again.

It must have been set off when he slammed the door shut after he had escorted that ungrateful wretch out of his house. *What a creep, calling his wife a witch, of all things. Didn't she know not to speak ill of the dead?*

He recalled that there was a key lying around somewhere. His wife used to wind that clock every so often and then stand next to it pleading hopefully, "Tick, pretty please!"

The old mechanism would give a muffled gong, move a minute or two, and then stall, making his diminutive wife steam up like a teapot.

It was her great-great-grandmother's, the only piece of her family history willed to her. The rest went to her brother, who married a Northerner and didn't disappoint the family.

That old clock was made by none other than George Mitchell of Bristol, Connecticut, at the beginning of the nineteenth century.

JB concentrated on the etching painted on the reverse glass of the case. It was a pastoral scene, with women holding parasols and men wearing pantaloons and beaver top hats. He noticed the mahogany case was layered with a coating of dust. He ran a crooked finger down the top, leaving a trail. *It's been neglected*, he thought and shook his head. His right knee twinged, and he chuckled, *like me*.

JB had seen many clocks like this one in his day. Despite its Yankee past, every family around here worth their salt had a similar one in their home, to be handed down through the ages.

Every family except his, perhaps.
His family had left him nothing.

JB grabbed a rag on the way to the living room, wiping the water rings from the surface of the coffee table. He'd given the victims of the car accident coasters, but they had carelessly placed them on the surface of the furniture. He'd made that piece for his wife from a tree felled by Hurricane Agnes in '72.

That tree had nearly killed them all, landing on the back of the cottage and taking out the kitchen and half of the dining room with it. JB had gotten his wife and kids out just in time, hiding in the underground root cellar until the worst of the storm had passed.

His eyes smarted now, and he swiped them with a gnarled hand, his loud sniff filling the silence.

He glanced up, blinking several times to clear his eyes, and focused on the picture of Ellie. He picked it up, his hand caressing the face, wishing he could feel her skin.

How dare she? he thought again, bitterly. *How dare that woman say his beloved was a witch?*

Ellie Straton was the sweetest woman to grace the earth, and JB missed her with every fiber of his being.

JB shut his eyes, too tired to think. His mind kept replaying the earlier part of the day over and over again.

He wanted to go back in time and ignore the sound of the blaring horn.

He could still recall the commotion outside that had interrupted his late-afternoon news program.

Grabbing a shotgun, he had thrown on an old sweater and navigated the rickety steps out of the cottage. He had struggled down the path leading to the main road, gripping his gun tightly.

A cold snap in the weather had made his old injury act up, slowing his movements and leaving him sleepless at night. Still, he had hefted the gun close since one couldn't be too careful. He had paused for a minute to give the clearing by the woods a good look. It was only yesterday he had seen a wolf lurking in a thicket at the end of his property.

He'd have to remember to tell the sheriff about it.

JB was sure that wolves were extinct in this part of Georgia.

At first, he had reckoned it might be a stray. He knew Bobby Ray and Trout Parker kept a pack of mongrels that annoyed most of the local farmers. Those mutts were known to raid the chicken houses, wreaking havoc on the best layers in the county.

He thought about the animal he had seen yesterday. *It could have been a dog.* He felt himself wavering. *No it was definitely a wolf.* He shook his head. *It was one big, bad-looking wolf.*

Frankly, he wasn't used to seeing much of anything on this side of town.

Most people stayed on the other end of Bulwark, especially since that smelly, green puddle had appeared out of nowhere.

He had reported stagnant water as soon as he had noticed it about ten days ago, but nobody cared.

It was on the Old Jericho Road that folks didn't travel anymore. Everyone knew the street had fallen out of use when the mill shut down years ago.

JB shook his craggy head. *People had no business traveling in that direction.* Strange stories had always come from that end of the county, even before he was born.

Some claimed spirits walked the woods and meadows; others said evil lurked there. Either way, from the time he was knee-high and the size of a tree stump, he knew to stay away.

Even talking about it gave him the willies, and that took a lot.

There was very little that frightened JB Straton, but for as long as he could remember, going into that neck of the woods was considered forbidden. Not that he believed in mumbo-jumbo. But somehow he had always taken those warnings seriously. *Damn, if he couldn't explain it, nobody could.*

JB Straton considered himself a rational man most of the time. However, there were those instances that gave him pause, especially with Ellie.

JB surveyed the growing pond filling the roadway, the shrill blast of the car horn making his heart beat a little faster in his chest. That sound could only mean someone was in trouble.

JB had looked for a source of the spreading water but didn't see where it started.

He knew the puddle was far from the creek that ran parallel to the back of his home. It was apparent it wasn't coming from there. Besides, that water was pure and clean, and this looked like sewage to him.

Only last week it had started as a puddle, and today, it looked like it had grown into a small pond, he grumbled. The smell was intolerable, the greenish color made it look like industrial waste.

Clay Finnes should have come earlier and investigated, he said to himself at the time.

He liked Clay well enough, had even voted for him. But maybe taking on the top job as sheriff was too much for the man. JB knew Clay was understaffed from budget cuts, and of course, there was that business about his child and his disintegrating marriage. *Sad stuff, kidnapping, right here in safe little Bulwark.*

Cries mixed with the discordant sound of the horn had brought him back to himself. JB slid down the embankment, landing in ankle-deep ooze.

He had slipped, catching himself but feeling the tight tendons on his leg protest. Cursing strangers, overgrown puddles, and his own bum knees, he had made his way resentfully toward the water. He had halted at the edge, considering his options.

A lone car, a Ford Fusion, was stuck in the middle of the quagmire. *City folk*, he muttered under his breath. Any sensible country person would never attempt to drive through deep water like that unless they had a truck.

A woman calf-deep in the water was trying to pull a man from the driver's side. JB shook his head grimly. The origin of the noise was her companion's head pressed against the steering wheel.

"Hey!" JB had called. "Hey, is everything okay?"

The stranger had looked in his direction, her eyes unfocused. She waved her hands. She was shouting something, but he could barely hear her.

He had squinted at her, turning his better ear in her direction to try to catch what she was saying.

She had screeched about her children and witches.

Witches? He had huffed. *Another nutjob looking for entertainment at the expense of the locals.* Last year, a film crew all the way from Hollywood had camped out on the edge of Sam Holsteam's farm, searching for the ghosts from a Civil War battle said to have occurred there.

The cast and crew had skedaddled quickly enough, screaming bloody murder. Everybody in town knew the film crew had left pasty-faced and hungover from Sam's peach moonshine. *City slickers*, he had snickered, *couldn't handle a good jug of 'shine.*

"Do you need help?" he had shouted to the woman.

This time, when she had looked at him, he had noticed a thin line of blood trickling from her hairline.

JB had patted his back pocket. He had hissed under his breath, calling himself five kinds of fool.

He'd forgotten that blasted cell phone his kid insisted he keep on him at all times in case he fell or something.

JB had bent awkwardly, placing the gun on the dry part of the incline and then gingerly stepping into the slimy puddle. He had realized that he had never changed into boots as his slippers filled with cold water.

Gritting his teeth, he had fought the urge to leave. *Why hadn't he removed the slippers?* Ellie had bought those slippers for him their last Christmas together. Now, they'd be ruined; his jaw twitched with resentment.

JB had waded toward the vehicle as the woman grew increasingly incoherent. As he had moved her out of the way, one of her flailing hands had caught him on the side of his head, and JB swore he heard bells ringing.

"No, stop it, woman. I'm here to help."

He had held her by both her shoulders, trying to reason with her, but she had looked as dazed as Johnny Gottfried had when he collided with a linebacker and suffered the worst concussion the NFL had ever recorded.

Her eyes had rolled in their sockets, and he saw her face drain of what little color it had. He had shaken her gently. "Now, don't go and faint on me, ma'am. I can't carry you both."

This had seemed to reach her, and she had whimpered.

She had grabbed the collar of his sweater, her bloody fingers poking holes in the fragile weave.

"My children . . . my children. Wicked, wicked place." She had looked like a wild woman, her mouth stretched in a soundless scream.

She had snagged a thread on his sweater when she grabbed him, loosening it. JB had watched it unravel and fought the urge to brush her away. *Ellie had knitted this sweater. How much more was this day going to cost him?*

JB had taken a steadying breath and then patiently turned the woman in the direction of his house. He had given her a poke to the center of her back. "Go there." He had pointed up the embankment. "I'll get your husband out."

He had watched her slog through the water to the other side, her head lowered.

Satisfied she was making progress, he had turned back to the man. His head rested against the steering wheel, his eyes were closed, and his skin had a faint bluish cast.

"Mister?" JB had called over the noise of the horn. He had touched the skin of the man's neck, recoiling at the clammy feel. This was not looking very good.

JB had wavered with the idea of moving him. He realized the water was now inching up over JB's thighs.

Again, he had looked for the source of the water, but had seen nothing except a widening greenish body of muck.

The door to the car was open and rapidly flooding with water. JB reached in, and using his upper body strength attempted to move the man. He couldn't budge him. JB placed his shoulder under the victim's arm and half dragged the man from the vehicle. He had been rewarded with a low groan, but the victim had definitely been nothing more than dead weight.

He had managed to get the couple into his cottage, wrap them both in blankets, and call the sheriff.

Tea with brandy had revived the wife enough for her to notice her surroundings.

It was then that she had focused on his Ellie's picture on the mantle and had accused his wife of stealing her children. Sheriff Clay Finnes had arrived just then, as his patience was wearing thin, along with that pushy news reporter Dayna Dalton. The injured couple was taken away, and he was left to the thick silence that felt like a comforting old blanket.

He was well rid of the intruders and now looked around his peaceful home, wishing his unwanted guests a speedy recovery along with the hope that he never had to set eyes on them again.

JB shuffled over to his recliner, his worn knees protesting.

He had changed his clothes after the whole hullabaloo but still felt chilled to the bone. *Took a long time to warm this old body*, he remembered ruefully.

He rubbed the skin of his thigh, the site of another football injury so horrible the bone had snapped and torn through his skin. *What was it, forty-four or forty-five years ago?*

He remembered waking from surgery, Ellie's hand brushing his forehead, her soft voice assuring him his football career had not ended.

He cleared his throat noisily, tears smarting his eyes, happy that Ellie wasn't here to witness it. *How dare that woman accuse his wife of being a witch? Not his Ellie, his soul mate, his life.*

JB settled into his chair, pulling the hand-knitted afghan over his knees. His head rolled, and with it, his memories unspooled like an old-time movie.

2

BULWARK, GEORGIA – 52 YEARS EARLIER

"I double-dare you!" Able Heston said, loud enough that JB was sure the entire cafeteria had heard.

"Shhhh, she'll hear you."

"So what? She should be the one quaking in her shoes. Go on, go ask her out." Able laughed loudly, slapping the table as if he'd heard something hilarious.

JB was sorry he had ever shared his interest in the new girl with Able.

Twice (or was it three times?), he had caught her looking straight at him, and he still wasn't sure that note in his locker was from her or was a practical joke instigated by Able.

"Stop it, Ab," JB grumbled. "You're acting like a jerk."

Able only laughed louder.

His friend turned to share his observations with the students at the table behind them.

JB tuned Able and the others out, refusing to let them rattle him. He had a game today and couldn't allow anything to unnerve him.

JB considered the new girl, wondering why he couldn't stop thinking about her.

Ellie Bronson was a blonde, blue-eyed beauty, newly arrived from Connecticut. She was a year younger than he was, same age as his kid sister, a junior to his senior. She had arrived later in the semester, starting school this past October.

Something had happened the day his eyes had met hers for the first time. It was like magic. He sucked in a breath, uncomfortable with the very idea.

Magic, he scoffed. *More like hormones.*

She was as graceful as a deer, he thought, watching her take her seat. Pretty, with clear skin and bright eyes.

Everybody made fun of her clipped Yankee accent. He thought it was sweet, musical-like. *Yikes*, he had to stop; he was making himself nauseous.

He didn't know why his eyes were always drawn to her like a magnet when she entered the room.

Aside from that, just the thought of her made him nervous, which he admitted was a new feeling. JB was quite the school heartthrob and never had an issue asking someone out. In fact, his sister Nancy teased that girls were lined up like he was the Piggly Wiggly and it was the day before Thanksgiving.

JB watched Ellie Bronson eating her lunch at a table in the corner. She was just a girl, a girl at school who was quieter and more reserved than any of the other females he'd grown up with these past eighteen years.

He'd been pinched by Cupid's bow, his sister had said when they were walking home the other day.

Well, he thought ruefully, he was asking for it. He wanted to slap himself on the side of the head after the questions left his stupid mouth. Looking back, he realized his clumsy inquiries had been pretty obvious.

"Did she say she had a boyfriend?" *What was he thinking?* He wanted to rip out his wayward tongue.

"Oh, you got it bad," Nancy had told him. "Really bad." She had pantomimed shooting an arrow with an imaginary bow, and he could have sworn the whole town had heard her yell, "Twang."

"Shut up!" He had looked around to see if anyone else had heard his sister's ribbing.

He had walked fast, leaving her in the dust, teasing that her big brother was in love with the new girl. Guess he deserved it for the frog he had put in her schoolbag last week.

Things had gotten stranger between him and the newcomer with each passing day.

While everyone knew he and Wanda Renfrew were practically a sealed deal, he found himself thinking less about Wanda and more about Ellie Bronson. No rest for him either when she invaded his dreams each night.

Strange dreams occurred, leaving him unsettled when he woke. Stranger still, because he could barely remember them.

Silly stuff, he scoffed, filled with ticking clocks and piano music from another time. He wasn't sure where or when the events of the dreams took place. The dreams faded as soon as sleep evaporated and dawn approached.

Since that first day he had seen Ellie, he knew he'd catch her watching him with those curious blue eyes if she were in the vicinity.

Ellie was everywhere he turned, whether it was in the gym or outside on the school steps. They kept bumping into each other. It was almost like fate itself was creating the ideal circumstances to shove them together. If he believed in fate, that is, and he assured himself that he didn't.

He could sense whenever she was in the area, before he even saw her. The hairs on the back of his neck would prickle, his scalp would tighten, and his skin would tingle. He could turn down a hallway from one class and watch as time slowed and the air chilled.

He knew as soon as the crowd cleared she'd be there, her eyes locked on his and her smile glowing like sunshine.

When he spotted her walking through those corridors, all sights and sounds faded, making him feel that they were alone in the world, as if no one else existed.

Everything muted to a gray blur, and he knew instinctively she'd been waiting for him and had been for a long time.

His well-ordered life had been turned upside down, and nowhere was safe.

He couldn't fight the feeling that he *knew* her. She felt as familiar as his hand or his face when he looked in the mirror. Common sense told him that was ridiculous, but something his grandmother had told him years ago gave it substance.

Even though he felt the very idea was impossible.

He was Georgia born and raised, and Ellie was from north of the Mason-Dixon line.

There was no connection, could never have been.

Still, he couldn't explain that sensation of *knowing*, as if they belonged together.

Granny had explained the feeling once on a cold night a few years before she died. JB recalled the discussion had happened the night he had gone someplace and felt he'd been there before or the time he'd looked at someone and recognized them even though they had never met. He told his grandmother about it, and she nodded, her wrinkled face splitting into a smile. "It's the *Knowing*. It's that feeling when you gonna meet your someone special," she had said, her dark eyes glittering.

"Oh, go on," he had laughed. He had dated a dozen girls and never felt anything remotely like that. He was going to stick with at least one of them, he had explained. After all, what were his options in Bulwark?

Now, in the lunchroom, he shuddered for a bit when the feeling swept over him. JB lowered his eyes, hoping nobody could guess what he was thinking.

Those strange thoughts skittered around in his head like a squirrel in a maple tree, always coming back to land on Ellie Bronson.

He'd heard her father was a transplanted executive who had moved down here when the automotive factory had opened in the fall.

JB rubbed his calloused hands together. He could see the red Georgia dirt embedded in the lines of the palms. He might be the best linebacker his high school had to offer, but that didn't take away the stain of his background.

What fancy, big-city girl would be interested in him?

He folded those calloused hands so the palms would stay hidden, his eyes following her movements around the room.

He compared her to the rest of the girls in the school. Ellie was so different.

He had known most of his classmates since they were babies.

People put down roots in Bulwark, Georgia, and stayed forever. He could name each family's parents and grandparents, maybe even a generation beyond that.

It had to be hard for her. JB watched her sitting alone.

The others hadn't welcomed her. It was bad enough she was a newcomer, but from *up north* as well.

Folks didn't like strangers in Bulwark. It was as if they'd lived in isolation for eons. Yes, the war had come in the 1860s, and they could even boast a small battlefield. But other than that bit of action, the world seemed to ignore this small corner of Georgia. There were whispers of strange goings on, witches and such, but JB knew they were just the folklore of country people, nothing more. The people of Bulwark were a close-mouthed lot, suspicious of strangers and content to hide inside the town's borders.

His cheeks tightening with shame, he remembered his father's rant the previous evening after his sister had brought up Ellie and her family at dinner. He was relieved that Nancy hadn't felt the need to share her suspicions that JB was sweet on Ellie.

"Damn Yankees, that's what they are! They should go back where they came from," his father had shouted, banging his fist on the table so the salt tipped over and spilled into a neat pile.

"Now, Leland, don't go on about that," his mother had said, placing a plate of fried chicken in front of him. "Don't matter much about them. It's not like they'll have anything to do with *us*."

She had sat down, holding her hands out for grace.

JB had squirmed in misery, hoping his sister didn't stir the pot by mentioning his crush, and so had been slow to take his mother's extended palm until a slap from his father to the back of his head made him jerk in his seat.

"Now, JB! You're holding up dinner. Probably mooning about the new girl. Pay attention, boy." His father had slammed his glass onto the table.

JB shifted uncomfortably in his seat, wanting to forget last night. His father was right; he wasn't paying attention. All he could think about was Ellie Bronson. She filled his thoughts at home, and now while he was sitting in the lunchroom at school too.

He squeezed his eyes shut, trying hard not to stare at Ellie, who was still sitting on the other side of the cafeteria. No matter what he did, he couldn't clear his mind.

Able elbowed him in the ribs. "Watch, watch. She's coming this way. Go on, ask her out. Go on."

He opened his eyes. It looked like Ellie was heading right for him.

"Ask her to the dance, I know you want to. You better do it this week, before someone else does."

JB felt his face flood with heat and his insides turn to jelly. For a minute his ears rang like the time he had crashed into the goalpost last semester. He ducked his head between his massive shoulders, wishing he could sink under the table.

Ellie had approached him yesterday to ask where the school newspaper's office was located. He had stuttered an answer, his tongue behaving as though it had a mind of its own.

He didn't know how she had located it with his stupid directions, but she must have asked someone else, since he had caught a glimpse of her leaving later, her books held close to her chest and a shy smile on her face.

Able spent the rest of the day imitating his stumbling reply to anyone who would listen.

Able was his best friend, and he was hard-pressed not to tell him off.

As his buddy tittered like a girl, JB fought the urge to punch him in his silly face. Everybody was looking at them. The lunchroom had gone strangely quiet.

JB stood unsteadily, all six feet, four inches of him, and murmured that he was late for his team meeting, his insides quivering with terror.

He gulped, wondering what frightened him so. Was it the fact that he was drawn to someone so different, or was he afraid of what his friends would think if he actually pursued her?

3

DOWN

JB didn't bother applying to college; it didn't matter because there wouldn't be any money to pay for it. His father expected him to work on the farm anyway. *Peanuts.* He hated the legumes.

"They pay good money for our crops. Keeps us from losing the farmstead," his father advised.

"It's like farming dirt," JB mumbled under his breath.

"What's that, boy?"

JB turned the television louder. "Game's on." Sunday was game day in the house. If a sport was on, JB and his dad were going to find it. That is, right after church.

Football was the only thing they could agree on. As long as they could share a game, peace reigned.

JB wished he could have made it to college on a scholarship, but he didn't even try. His parents were never going to let him go. He was the only son, and his place was at home, helping to work the fields.

Practice was every afternoon after school. His parents didn't fuss much as long as he did his chores first thing in the morning. It was a grueling day, waking before four to shovel crap around and milk the cows, but there was nothing he could do about it. He had responsibilities. His mind wandered as he recalled last Thursday.

The coach had motioned to him when they had finished practice. "Meet me in the office after you've changed."

JB had nodded and raced to the lockers, wondering if he was in trouble for something.

Coach had looked up when he had entered the small room. "Sit down, JB."

JB had sat down on the chair opposite the coach. His legs were pressed right up to the metal desk, his sore knees aching.

Coach had opened a drawer and pulled out a thick envelope, sliding it across the desk.

JB had stared at the red crest emblazoned on the front, his body frozen, his breath hitching in his chest.

He'd cleared his throat. "Um . . . what's that?"

"Application to Bama. Take it home and fill it out."

JB hadn't moved. Sweat had dotted his upper lip. He'd swiped at it, his face as red as the ink on the return address on the envelope.

"Take it, go on," the coach had urged.

JB had reached out and held the envelope reverently, the crest of the University of Alabama embellished on the front.

"Yep, the Crimson Tide. Bear's called me about you."

"Bear Bryant?" JB had whispered in awe. He'd gulped, sitting back in his chair. "Thank you, sir, but I can't."

"I'm not taking no for an answer, son. You got to fill it out." The coach had pounded the surface of his desk with his blunt finger.

"Can't. My daddy would kill me."

Coach had taken his hat off and thrown it on his desk. He'd wiped his bald head with a handkerchief that he'd pulled from his back pocket. For a minute, the older man had stared out of the gated windows, his jaw working furiously. When he spoke, JB had been surprised to see that the coach had tears in his eyes.

"You got a rare talent, JB, that can't be wasted. Out there on the field today, you led that team. You think on your feet, better'n anybody I ever taught." The coach had sat up. "You're not like those other meatheads. I would be remiss as your coach if I didn't make you try. You're going to be a star one day."

JB had looked at the brown envelope. *A star*. A football star, not a peanut farmer, and the chance to go to college. He'd like that. He'd imagined walking up to Ellie's house wearing a lettered sweater. *No, she'd be wearing his sweater*. He'd be a college boy, not a dirt-poor farmer.

"Go on, now. Put down your information. I'll help you fill the dang thing out if you need me to."

JB had looked around the office. No one but he and the coach needed to know. He'd indulge this fantasy, just once.

"There's no money . . ."

"Don't worry 'bout it, JB. Just fill out the form." The coach had held out a fancy pen with a white star on the point. He'd smiled and touched the tip. "My folks bought me this pen when I graduated Georgia Tech. Use it. Use it for good luck."

JB had taken the pen. It'd been heavy in his hand. It was a suitable tool for doing something as important as this.

JB had looked at the first line and then twisted the pen so that the ink tip popped out. He'd written his name in bold letters. It didn't hurt to dream, he'd shrugged. He knew he'd never get accepted to the school; there was no money to pay for it anyway. *What was the harm in trying?*

JB had finished the forms and left the office, promptly forgetting about enrolling into college, when he saw Ellie strolling home from school. All thoughts had fled from his head then.

He had slowed his truck, warring with the idea of asking if she wanted a ride. He could swear he'd caught her looking at him. He'd peered hard at her, but she'd never turned her head. JB had struggled with indecision. Should he tap the horn, or would she think he was an uncouth farmer? He'd rolled down the window, but the words had stuck in his throat. *What should he say? Do you need a ride? Nah? Can I give you a lift?* He'd cleared his throat and opened his mouth. What if she didn't want a ride? Maybe she wanted to be by herself. She looked lonely, he'd thought. Her face was downcast, and he'd willed her to look up to see him. She hadn't; her chin remaining glued to the stack of books she carried in her arms. A horn had honked impatiently behind him, and he had taken off without saying a word.

The following Tuesday, JB had put on his uniform and jogged from the locker room toward the field. He held his helmet loosely in his hand, the fading daylight warming his face.

He didn't see Ellie so much as sense her when she stepped from under the bleachers. He had to admit that, while he wasn't surprised, he did feel nervous.

"You keep avoiding me," she said, as she stood before him, her books held protectively before her. The sun gilded her hair and kissed her cheeks. Lilies of the Valley wafted over him. He knew at once he'd associate that fragrance with her forever more.

She licked her bottom lip, and JB couldn't help the sigh that escaped him. "I saw you watching me from your truck last week. You could have offered me a lift."

"I don't know what you're talking about," he answered, his face flushing.

"Oh, don't you? I've tried everything. I've attempted conversations with you. I've gone to every game. I even pushed a note through your locker."

JB shuffled his feet. "Yeah, I know."

"Then what's the problem?"

JB placed a hand on his hips. "Look," he paused trying to find a way to be sensible. "I'm from the wrong side of town."

"That's so cliché." She smiled, revealing her perfect white teeth. "That may have mattered in the last decade, but it's the sixties now. People don't care about those things."

"Your father will," he blurted.

Ellie lowered the books, her face softening. "You don't know that."

JB's breath caught in his throat. She was so beautiful, her eyes luminous. The college form flashed in his brain, but he refrained from mentioning it. It wouldn't matter, even if he got accepted to the school; there was no money to actually go there. His face turned bleak.

"I have no future. I'm the son of a farmer, and that's what I'm going to be. Look, I have to go."

She placed her hand on his arm.

As her warm palm caressed his skin, sparks tingled through his bloodstream. He breathed deeply, wanting nothing more than to throw down his helmet and kiss her right there in the open where everybody would see. *But he didn't.* He shook his head.

Ellie stamped her foot on the ground, and JB couldn't help but smile. She looked like a fierce kitten. "I am determined to go out with you, JB Straton!"

JB cocked his head, his chest filling with hope. "I don't know why."

Ellie moved closer then, so close that he could breathe in her scent. "Sometimes, there is no *why* in these things." Her voice was low. The shouts from his friends on the field faded, and the air stilled between them. "I knew it from the minute I saw you. You were meant for me. Did *you* ever feel that, like you've known someone your whole life even though you just met them?" She touched him again, her small hand caressing the space where his heart beat like a trapped bird. "I know you feel it too."

The world narrowed to just the two of them, and JB felt like no one else existed. North and South be damned, he wanted to hold her.

JB dropped his helmet with a groan. He pulled her to him. Her books tumbled from her arms and scattered on the grass. Cocking his head, he touched her lips with his own, the thrill of skin on skin shooting through him like fireworks. She whimpered, her eyes closing as she kissed him back. They fit together like two puzzle pieces or a key that had finally found the right lock. Something unfurled within him, rushing through his bloodstream.

It was the best feeling in the world, better than anything he'd ever experienced. He knew he had loved this girl for longer than time, but couldn't understand how or *why*.

"Sometimes, we don't have choices in life. We have to follow our heart," Ellie whispered, her voice a sweet caress.

"I don't have choices at all," he said to her.

They kissed again, her lips pliant and soft under his. His body was hard against hers. He wanted to surround her. Almost like a dance, they moved into the shadow of the bleachers, kissing hungrily at first and then slowing down to savor the moment. Time stopped. His hands moved up and down her back while hers slid under his shirt, driving him mad with desire.

She rested her head against his chest. He felt strong and protective of her.

"Did it ever occur to you that I was *meant* to move here, just to meet you?" She looked up at him, their eyes locking. An atom bomb could have gone off around him, and JB wouldn't have noticed. There was only Ellie, and it felt *right* to hold her in his arms. He never wanted to let her go.

"I've waited forever for this," she said.

JB nodded in agreement. He was sure he had waited just as long.

He looked into her eyes and did the only thing he could think to do. He kissed her again.

4

BLITZ

They met secretly since he knew her parents wouldn't approve. They got to know each other's bodies well. He kissed all parts of her, her collarbone, the spot behind her ear, her breasts, the flat of her stomach. He couldn't believe he could kiss someone for as many hours as he did with Ellie.

He teased her about her accent, and she made fun of his real name.

She was bold in exploring his muscular frame, with a sense of possession laced with familiarity.

While he had done more things with other girls, this felt different; sometimes, his hands shook in his eagerness, slowing reverently as his fingers remembered the dips and valleys of her skin. He took his time, finally realizing the difference between kissing and lusting after somebody.

His rusty old truck had a roomy bench seat where they often lay stretched out together, stealing time after school.

Whenever she left, her essence, the fragrance of lilies, remained for the rest of the day, as though it had absorbed into his skin.

Football season was over now, and he had maybe an hour to spare before he needed to be home. Ellie told her parents she stayed for tutoring or was at a friend's doing homework.

"I'd like you to meet my parents," she told him one day.

JB was shirtless, his hands behind his head. She caressed the flat plane of his stomach, stopping short at his belt buckle. "Not a good idea," he said.

For a minute, he caught her looking up at him, a question in her eyes, and he laughed, taking her hand to his lips.

"Oh, you mean my parents," she said. "It will be alright. You don't understand them."

She tried to persuade him by saying that they were nice people and would welcome him with open arms. JB laughed when she said that and told her she was naive.

The problem was that he knew in his gut that her father would not be happy. But, at the same time, he wasn't pleased to be skulking around and hiding their budding relationship. Still, he refused to go, and Ellie firmed her lips to finish the discussion another day.

JB headed for his pickup after school one day in the spring. It was a '56 Chevy, and he'd asked Emmet Harding to paint it red in exchange for rebuilding a chicken coop. Took them both one whole Saturday and half of a Sunday to do it. He touched the shiny surface, proud of the old truck.

He knew he didn't have to be ashamed of it now.

He had just thrown his books and jacket over the tailgate, whistling as he walked, when he felt a hard blow to the side of his head.

JB was big, but he was unprepared for the blow, and he went down hard, landing on his side.

Someone kicked him then. The world spun dizzily on its axis. A fist glanced off his cheek and then came down again, hitting him squarely in the eye.

JB scrambled to his feet, realizing he was surrounded.

They were older, not from around here. One wore a leather jacket from the University of South Carolina. He didn't recognize them. He squared off with a tall blonde guy who looked vaguely familiar.

"Stay away from Ellie, trash," his opponent spit out.

JB took a swing at his aggressor, hitting him squarely on the jaw and rocking the other man on his heels. That punch would have felled most guys. While JB saw that he'd done some damage, his challenger still stepped forward agilely, jamming him in the solar plexus. This dude was quick on his feet, jabbing like a welterweight boxer. It was apparent that he had trained. JB swatted at him as if he were a mosquito, but his rival ducked and punched with lightning-quick darts.

The man knocked JB's wind from him. He doubled over wheezing as he tried to regain his breath. He was sure that he'd cracked a rib.

Two other men yanked JB up, grabbing his arms and holding him while the blonde hammered away.

"This is your only warning. Stay away from my sister."

Something connected with the back of his head, and all went black.

The rapid staccato of multiple shots penetrated JB's consciousness. *Gunshots? Was it hunting season?* He was flat on his back and for a minute couldn't remember where he was. He shook his head and the pain made him black out again. It was dark when JB opened his eyes. He felt like he'd slept for hours. He choked on the smoke, not understanding where it was coming from. It was different that a campfire, with sulfurous odor he associated with gun powder. Cracking his eyes open carefully, he peered through the thick haze. He shook his head groggily, setting off a ringing that nearly split his skull.

He cradled his head, rolling over. Pain shot up his leg from ankle to hip. He was wet; his uniform stuck to his body. Rain dripped from the leafy trees above him, sending shivers down his spine.

JB looked down to see a butternut jacket hanging loosely on his thin form. His boots were gone, his feet covered in rags. His musket was underneath him. JB knew only one thing: he had to move out of the line of fire. He tucked the gun close to his battered body and began to crawl in the mud.

Shots rang out around him. His head cleared, and he knew the battle was nearing the end. He looked at Bobby Parker's body sprawled by a tree stump. Bobby's cousin Raymond lay dead on the other side of the clearing. He called two names, one a captain's and the other another soldier's, the words coming without thinking. For a moment, he wondered dizzily how he remembered those names when he could barely remember his own. The other troops melted into the woods, overpowered by the Union forces, leaving him for dead.

JB squeezed his eyes, trying to remember the last few hours, but he drew a blank, as though he'd been dropped into this spot out of thin air. For a minute, he couldn't remember where he came from. Then, his brain cleared.

They'd been on patrol near Bulwark, his hometown. For most of the war, he'd been in areas farther north. But with each loss, his unit had retreated, eventually skirting his homestead earlier today.

He was on picket patrol with those idiot Parker boys. He'd known them since they were babies. He paused, wondering why he knew that. His wits sharpened, and it all came back with a tidal force.

They had stumbled upon a Union scouting party, and with dwindling ammo, it didn't take long for the enemy to decimate them. The Yankees made off with their horses, leaving the Rebels to die in the red Georgia mud.

He bit back a cough, his head swam, and he realized he was bleeding. Closing his eyes, he breathed deeply, waiting for his strength to come back so he could struggle to his feet and get out of there.

He might have lain there for two minutes or two hours, he couldn't tell.

Everything was fuzzy when he opened his eyes again. He fought the urge to drift off, instead grabbing handfuls of grass as he tried to pull himself under the safety of a bush.

He heard a rustle, rolled over, and aimed his gun, knowing even then that it was futile. He was a dead man.

His gun was empty. Even if he had bullets, he didn't have the strength to load them. But dammit, JB Straton would go out in a blaze of glory!

"Hush!" It was a woman's voice.

JB's eyes opened wide. It was vaguely familiar and decidedly female.

He saw a shadow groping through the thicket. "No, don't shoot. It's me. I've been watching from the cabin."

She scrambled over to him on her hands and knees.

A fragrance wafted over him; it was light and summery. "I smell lilies."

"Don't worry; you're not dead yet." He could hear the smile in her voice.

He blinked at her small form. She had a shawl covering her hair, but he could discern huge blue eyes when she leaned over him, rain dripping down her face.

"I know you," he said softly.

"Of course, you know me, JB Straton. We've gone to every barbecue and family picnic together our whole lives."

"No, you . . . you . . . don't come from here."

"Shush. You hit your head?" Gentle fingers sifted through his hair, making his scalp tingle with pleasure. He groaned.

A shot rang out, and the girl threw herself over him, rolling them both under the bushes.

"I thought those fools left," she said grumpily.

They lay together for a long while, their breathing almost synchronized. "Don't you leave me now, JB. Stay with me," she whispered. He smiled at the concern in her voice.

The shouts grew fainter, JB thought dully. He opened his mouth to say something but felt a cool hand over his lips. JB kissed her fingers, and he could feel her letting out a sigh of relief.

He opened his eyes lazily to see her mouth curve into a smile.

"Your timing has always been off, JB," she whispered.

She waited for a bit and then lifted her head. "They're gone for good, now. No, don't move, you big looby. Let me see your wound."

"Who are you, really?" his voice croaked.

She looked at him, her face hurt, her expression folding inward. She cupped his cheek tenderly. "Don't speak now."

The rain slowed, letting a watery sun peek through the clouds. JB squinted.

She tugged off her shawl and used it to make a tourniquet on his leg. He grunted from the pain.

"I know it hurts, but we have to stop the bleeding."

As she looked down at him, JB reached a hand weakly to touch her face. She was surrounded by sunlight, her hair a sparkling halo around her head.

"You're an angel," he said. The world had a sepia glow as if he were caught in some old picture from another time.

"Hardly," she laughed, a silvery sound that vibrated throughout his body.

He recognized that laugh, but couldn't place it. "No, no. You're not from around here."

She frowned. "It doesn't matter. You're here, and I'm here; that's all that counts now." His eyes slid shut.

JB awoke to a cool cloth resting on his head. He was in a dimly lit room he didn't recognize.

"Don't get up just yet, unless you want to land on the floor," an older woman's voice said.

JB didn't listen. He saw a stranger standing by a window and felt a moment of confusion. He touched his chest and felt his tattered T-shirt. Colors were no longer hazy or muted. He was in his own clothes and not caught in some mysterious realm. He let his head fall back on the pillow with relief.

The room swam, and nausea assaulted him when he attempted to focus his eyes. He knew he was here with Ellie. He didn't need to look for her; the room was filled with the scent of lilies.

"I dreamt . . . I dreamt . . ." He couldn't form a sentence.

"I know what you dreamt. I had that dream too," Ellie said, her voice sounding far away.

He tried to lock on her face. He felt her fingers squeeze his hand.

JB met Ellie's eyes. They both looked at the other person in the room. The woman stood by the window, staring through the lace curtains out to the street, her expression bleak.

"Who is that?" he asked, his voice cracked.

"Rosalie Scott." Ellie held a glass of water to his lips, gently cupping the back of his head to help him drink.

The fresh water revived him a bit. It dripped down his chin, and she wiped it tenderly.

"Henry Scott's wife," Ellie informed him.

JB closed his eyes. The Scotts lived near the school. Tragedy had touched them, leaving a mark of sorrow on the woman's face. Her child had been stolen from her bed last winter, never to be seen again. They said Mrs. Scott went mad and roamed the meadows and forests calling out for the little girl. Now, she was resting her hand on her bulging belly protectively.

"She's been very nice. She found you and managed to drag you to her home. Do you remember telling her to call me?"

"I did?" He half sat up, and the room spun.

"You even gave her my number. Don't move, you big looby." Ellie pushed him down.

"What?" he asked, knowing he'd heard those words in another time. "What did you say? Did you call me that before?"

"You big looby? No, you were too busy talking up a storm about Rebel uniforms, battles, and wounds. You spoke a lot in your sleep."

"Just a dream," he said, his head falling back weakly on the pillow. He was drained. His heart raced, and a wave of panic assaulted him, making his skin crawl. He shifted nervously.

"But it felt so real, didn't it?" Rosalie Scott added, then turned to look out the window again.

JB ignored the other woman. She was giving him a serious case of the creeps, staring out the window while she talked to them. "Ellie? You shouldn't be here." he said.

"It was my brother, wasn't it?" Ellie asked.

JB swallowed. It hurt to talk. He nodded once. "He's only trying to protect you."

"He's an animal!" she said through gritted teeth.

"I'd do the same thing if you were my sister."

"I don't believe you for a minute, JB. You wouldn't judge a person based on their position in society or how much money they had."

"I can't fight your family. They only want what's best for you."

Ellie leaned against him, her hands entwined with his. "I know what's best for me. You're what's best for me."

"Ellie." He sat up with a wince. He felt his strength returning. "I can't give you the life they want for you, that you deserve."

"Don't tell me what I deserve, JB. You're good and kind. I love you." She moved closer to him on the bed. JB could feel the softness of her hip next to his. She caressed his face, her eyes tender. "I don't want anything but you. I don't care if we live in a shack or a mean little cabin in the woods as long as I can be with you. You know it's where I belong."

Rosalie looked at them from the window. "Best you be goin' now."

JB rolled his legs off the bed with a groan. Ellie helped him with his sneakers. He was sore but had suffered no real damage; he felt as if he had played tackle with a rough group of guys. As long as he could move, JB knew his ribs were bruised, but not broken. Gathering his things, he took hold of Ellie's hand.

"I have to go back for my truck," he told her.

"I'll come with you."

"It's getting late." He shook his head.

"My parents think I'm doing homework with Donna. We'll be fine."

"What about your brother?"

Ellie shrugged. "I knew he came in for the day. He was going back to school this afternoon. He should be on his way to Carolina by now."

They left, walking hand in hand toward the high school to retrieve his vehicle.

Crickets chirped in the gathering gloom. The air had cooled a bit. JB put his arm around

Ellie's shoulders, holding her close. They reached the corner, a deserted intersection near the school. Ellie nuzzled her face against his chest, making JB's heart beat a new rhythm. JB leaned over to kiss her.

His lip hurt, and he must have made a noise. Ellie kissed his neck and wrapped her arms tightly around his shoulders.

"Let's go to the truck," she said between kisses.

"You have to get home," JB said pulling her arms down and moving away. He took her hand, striding faster toward the vehicle. "I'll drive you home," he said. He opened the passenger door for her to get in. Ellie pushed it shut.

She pulled his face down, kissing him, her mouth open, her tongue dancing with his. There was a new urgency in her kisses, as if she needed to be as close to him as possible.

"I was so scared when I first saw you. I wanted to call the police, but Mrs. Scott said it was just a good drubbing. She said you'd be okay and that, if you knew anyone from Bulwark, they wouldn't want to involve the sheriff."

JB simply kissed her back. "I'm fine."

Ellie sucked on his lower lip; she couldn't get enough of him.

JB kissed her deeply, meeting each thrust of her tongue with his own, twining both together.

They moved blindly, banging into the side of the truck. He pressed Ellie against the metal, his hips caressing hers.

JB was on fire, his being devoured by Ellie. His breath came in short pants while Ellie whimpered. Her fingers fumbled with his belt buckle, and he pushed her hands away. This was taking it to a new level. JB stopped kissing her, resting his forehead against hers and breathing as if he had just returned an eighty-yard interception. "Don't."

"Why?" she asked, her face flushed.

"I won't be able to stop," he whispered.

Ellie put her trembling fingers over his lips. He fought the urge to suck on them.

"I don't care." She reached under his belt, her fingers surrounding him, gripping him. JB gasped, his body emptied of air. His hands ran up and down her back, cupping her behind. He lifted her, pressing her against him so she could feel what she was doing to him.

Despite his sore muscles, he reached for the handle and opened the door of the truck. He lifted Ellie in, sliding her backward onto the seat. He lay heavily on top of her, their breathing harsh as if they'd run a race.

"You sure you want to do this?" He kissed her lips reverently. "Tell me no now or—" he stopped, his chest heaving. He made a movement as if he were getting up.

Ellie pulled him to her, grinding her hips against his. He slid his hand down her flank and under her dress, then up her thigh to rest on her mound. "I love you, Ellie."

Ellie ran her fingers through his hair, kissing him deeply. He heard her breathe yes into his ear. JB reached backward, pulling the door closed behind them.

5

HAIL MARY

His mother sat at the table, a cigarette dangling from her fingers, her face set.

She glanced at him when he walked through the door. She jumped up and moved closer, grabbing him by the shirt. "Took you long enough to get home." She looked at his bruised face. "You been in a scuffle," she hissed, her voice low.

"No, ma'am." JB ducked his head so she wouldn't see the worst of it. "Got into a tussle romping around with Able and the guys."

She pursed her lips, and he knew she didn't believe him. "Your father ain't gonna be happy," she added flatly.

"That's nothing new." JB dropped his books onto the floor, realizing belatedly that they weren't alone. Someone was sitting on the couch.

"We have company," his mother said. Her voice was tight.

She moved out of the way, and the air *whooshed* out of JB's chest as if he had been coldcocked.

He moved to the couch on rubbery legs, lowering himself on the other side of the plaid sofa.

Bear Bryant sat with his ever-present houndstooth fedora balanced on his knee, watching him intently.

"Must have been quite a tussle," he said, his eyes taking in JB with a knowing look. It felt like Bryant could see through him, inside and out.

Bear Bryant had a deep voice, and JB understood in an instant that team members would follow his commands to the end of the earth.

Bryant put out his right hand. "I think we've established you know who I am." He smiled then with a rare ease that lit up the room. "Believe me, son. I know who you are too."

JB wiped his palm down his dirty jeans. "Yes, sir." He looked at his mother.

"You applied to Bama?" Her stance made it an accusation.

JB winced, wishing she wouldn't look so hurt.

"Huh," JB stuttered, sweat breaking out on his forehead. The room swam for a minute, but he knew it wasn't from the beating he'd taken. He heard the back door slam, dread filling him when his father walked into the room.

Leland Straton stomped into the parlor, his dung-coated boots leaving a mess on the floor. "I saw a car outside. Who'd be coming at this . . . ?"

Leland looked from JB to Bear Bryant, standing there while he wiped his hands on a filthy rag.

He shook his head, "Nope. Ain't gonna happen."

JB watched Bryant assess his father and nod. "Full scholarship. Boy's gonna make something of his life."

Leland pulled a chair from the dining area, straddled it, and then sat down. "I'll lose him for four years, and he won't make anything, not a damn dime. Besides, you can't teach him how to grow peanuts," he said fiercely.

Bear Bryant nodded as if he understood Leland's argument. JB held his breathe. This day was growing more eventful with each passing second.

Bear Bryant and JB's father quietly stared at each other as if they were bulls in a pen, sizing up their opponents. JB looked at his mother. *Jeez*, her nostrils were flared like a mare in heat. He leaned up against the wall, well out of everyone's way.

"I'll treat him like my son." Bryant broke the charged silence.

His mother sobbed then. JB's heart lurched from the sound. It was as if she knew she had lost him already.

Her eyes filled, and she bit a work-reddened knuckle.

Leland threw her a dirty look, cocking his head toward the kitchen. She rose. "I've got some gravy and biscuits."

"I would love that, Missus Straton."

"Call me Jean."

Bryant nodded.

JB could see his father's face was set.

"Education is a great opportunity."

"Education is for the rich to get richer."

Bear Bryant paused and looked straight at JB's father. "I know you want what's best for your son," he said slowly. His voice was low, reasonable. "I know . . ." Bear paused. "I know you want him to have a better life." His sharp eyes darted around the sparse farmhouse. JB could see them rest on the ratty carpet, worn couch, and uneven floors. "Besides, by the time he's done, he's going to be able to help y'all."

"Football players?" Leland asked. "They make big money?"

"Some do. Some don't." Bryant's eyes were locked on his father's. "I know this boy is going to make a difference."

"Difference don't pay the bills."

"Does when I say so," Bryant finished.

For a minute there was nothing but silence in the room.

"You're going to be proud of your boy."

Leland stiffened as if he'd been slapped. JB saw his father swallow hard and then sag with defeat.

"I don't have nothin' . . . nothin' to help."

Bryant sat up, his elbows on his knees. "You don't need nothin,' Lee. May I call you Lee? I told you I will treat him like my son.

6

BOOTLEG

"I'm not real sure about this," his father said after Bear Bryant left. "I say he's full of shit."

JB heard dishes clatter in the sink. Nancy cleared the rest of the table and then joined her mother in the kitchen.

"Dad . . . he's right outside the door. Bear Bryant's word is like gold," JB replied in reverent tones, afraid Bryant might have caught his father's comment when he left.

"Shut your mouth. You don't understand anything, boy." His father pulled out a bottle of 'shine and poured himself half a glass. "He probably forgot about you the minute he walked outta here." He took a swig and shivered.

JB looked outside the farmhouse, the porch light illuminating their visitor as he slid into his car.

JB saw the outline of the famous hat on his head. Bear didn't once look back at the house. Soon, all that was left was a trail of dust.

"He came all that way for JB," his mother walked in from the kitchen, drying a plate.

"All that way," Leland scoffed. "Georgia football players are a dime a dozen." He pointed a grimy finger in JB's direction. "I hear one whiff of you braggin' 'bout this, and you're gonna be lookin' for your teeth in yonder field." He swallowed the rest of the glass in one gulp, slamming it on the side table, and then belched loudly. "You don't say nuthin' to nobody till your bags are packed and you're on the way to Bama. Ain't nobody gonna embarrass me. Not Bear Bryant and certainly not you."

At night, in his bedroom, JB lay flat on his back exhausted, a stupid grin on his face. It didn't matter that this day had begun as the worst of his life. Between getting the crap kicked out of him by Ellie's brother, and that weird fantasy of a Civil War battle, the day couldn't have been stranger. The highs and lows of meeting Ellie in his dreams, and in the present were surreal. He wasn't sure where the line of reality began or ended. Then the monumental capping the day with Bear Bryant was perfection. It had truly ended up being the best in his life. JB was feeling on top of the world. He traced a pattern on the pillow, wishing she was next to him.

He rolled over, content that his life was in order. He would hold the exciting information close to his chest, for now. He smiled, thinking about Ellie's face when he could finally tell her the news. He would have to wait until things were really set in motion and there would be no going back. He couldn't wait to see her reaction.

Their prospects were on an upswing. In four years, he'd be qualified to get a job that could support her the way she deserved. No matter what it took, JB was going to be successful, like Ellie's father.

7

SKIRMISH

"I don't understand." Ellie faced him, her face awash with tears. They were in her father's study.

Her parents had left for a business trip, and Rosalie Scott had been sleeping at the Bronson's for the past two days as a chaperone to take care of Ellie.

School was days away from ending. JB had waited until he felt he could wait no more. He finally told Ellie the news about Alabama. For some reason, she didn't seem as thrilled as he was with the idea.

JB looked at the antique clock on the wall, which was frozen at five o'clock. He'd been to visit Ellie several times during the weekend, and the time had never changed. Ellie had told him that it was an old piece of junk and hadn't worked right since they had moved to the South. There was a key somewhere, Ellie had shrugged, but it was a temperamental timepiece.

"Lotta things don't work right in Bulwark," Rosalie said, catching the direction of JB's gaze from the doorjamb, where she watched the couple intently.

"Can we have a minute, Mrs. Scott?" Ellie said, bordering on rudeness.

While they managed a fair share of privacy in JB's truck, they wouldn't dare try anything at Ellie's house.

Rosalie Scott pushed herself from the wall. "Your parents will be mad at me that I let him in." Before she turned to leave, she looked straight into JB's eyes, muttering, "Enough kids done disappeared round here, already. Don't need two more."

JB rolled his eyes wondering what the heck she was talking about. She was a batty old thing, more so since her baby had been born.

Ellie waited until she left, then pressed herself against him. He could feel her body shaking. "I can't believe you didn't tell me." Her blue eyes looked hurt, and she gnawed her lower lip.

Guilt washed over JB. "I didn't want to hide it from you. Much as I hate to admit it, my father might have been right, and Bryant could have been full of hot air."

He took both her hands in his. "He wasn't, and now I actually have a future. You won't have to be ashamed to be my wife."

"Let's run away tonight," she pleaded. "We can get married."

JB shook his head, a tender smile on his face.

"Yes, we can. I'm a year over the legal limit," Ellie persisted.

"With parental consent," JB interrupted her. He took her face in his hands and stared into her eyes. "I love you with all my heart, but I want more for you."

"JB!" Ellie said impatiently. "More for me? I don't need anything else but you." A fat tear rolled from the corner of one of her eyes. Another hung from her dark lashes. JB could feel the heat of her skin as if she were burning with fever.

The clock on the wall chimed, making them both jump. "I thought that thing never worked," JB said with a mirthless laugh. This was not going the way he expected.

"It doesn't. It's ringing now to tell you time is running out." Ellie turned away from him, her shoulders stiff.

"You don't believe that, Ellie," he said softly, kissing her lightly on the back of her neck. She shoved him away with her shoulder.

"I do. I'll believe anything that will knock some sense into that stubborn head of yours." She sounded mulish.

"It'll just be for four years. We'll write and visit each other, I promise."

Ellie sobbed, her chest heaving. She spun and clung to him like a lifeline. "You won't. You'll find a new girl, some pretty Southern girl and—"

"You're the only girl I want," he whispered, raining kisses on her cheeks and nose. "I won't even look at anybody else, I swear."

Ellie pushed him away. "You say that now." She folded her arms over her chest and then slid her hands down to cover her belly.

A wall went up between them.

JB could see her hurt and anger take over. His kitten had claws. He picked up his truck keys. "I love you, girl. There won't ever be another. I'll write every day." JB gathered his things, stopping at the door. "I'll be leaving on Tuesday. I'd like to see you again before I go."

Ellie shrugged one shoulder.

"Ellie . . ."

"Just go."

They didn't see each other. JB left sad and confused and didn't write for the first three weeks. Finally, he gave in and penned a long, rambling letter telling Ellie what she meant to him.

She wrote him once. It wasn't even a response to his note. The letters crossed in the mail. Her language was cool. She'd been accepted for early admissions to a college in

Pennsylvania, and he could tell she was still simmering about their separation. Still, he wrote her diligently, his hurt growing when she failed to reply.

Time was at a premium, and while Coach Bryant was true to his words and treated him as a son, JB had to work harder and longer than anyone else in the school. He took on a job cleaning equipment, sending most of his earnings home to help his parents. On long weekends, he stayed at school. He didn't want to go home, even if he had the time. Ellie's abandonment tortured him.

So he stayed, helping the janitorial staff and making extra money.

Despite how busy he was, he spent hours writing her about practice, his classes, and his meets. He gave her dates of the upcoming games he'd play in Georgia, but she never showed up or even wrote back. By December, he stopped writing.

He lost weight, not from working out, but because food tasted like dust in his mouth. He toyed with going home but knew that, if he left, there'd be no going back. He had responsibilities. He knew that wasn't the real reason. He was afraid to hear what Ellie might say.

JB finally gave in and asked his sister to talk to Ellie, see if she could plead his case.

Nancy wrote back immediately. She thought he knew. The Bronsons had left

Bulwark soon after the school term started. They had moved away, forwarding address unknown.

JB crumpled the note he was writing to Ellie, his face tight with shame. She hadn't told him the school where she was going. She was lost to him, forever.

8

ENCROACHMENT

It's amazing what the body can accomplish with a broken heart. JB applied all his energy to school, discovering that he had a knack for engineering and majoring in physics. He ended up gradating with honors. He worked at a lab part-time, managing to put away quite a bit of his earnings.

He poured his soul into studying. His heart was too sore to attempt dating until his junior year, when Linda Westerly caught his eye and he cautiously rejoined the dating pool.

Linda led to Betty Ann. Betty Ann ended when he met Sondra. Soon, he had a reputation as a fun but fickle lover.

He enjoyed the company of these women, but no matter what they tried, not one girl managed to pierce the hardened armor of his heart.

Over the years, he'd approached some of Ellie's acquaintances in Bulwark, asking casual questions to see if anybody had heard from her.

It was as if she had never lived there. JB wondered if he had imagined her existence like the nagging Civil War nightmares that plagued his sleep.

The nightmares were always the same. He was wounded, and Ellie rescued him. He'd always wake up shaking and frozen in fear, once or twice even screaming, afraid to let the nightmare continue.

In his senior year, the dreams had stopped. The last one had ended the night after a curious incident.

JB had been at an away game at Penn State. It was the second quarter, and Penn State had the ball. JB came out of a team huddle, and a shiver raced up his spine.

The sound of the crowd dulled, as though his head were covered by a bag. He felt his muscles twitch and his neck grow hot. He turned, scanning the bleachers. The roar of the fans faded as his eyes searched the seats.

To say he felt like he was being watched sounded dumb to his own ears, but he felt a difference in the air.

"Where are you?" he whispered. She was there, in the crowd. He knew it down to his bones, but he couldn't find her in the thousands of faces filling the stadium.

He turned in a circle.

"JB!" the cornerback yelled. "What? You get hit in the head or something?"

JB shook his head but didn't take his eyes off the crowd.

"JB! Now!"

He ran to his position and played the rest of the game, but knew neither his heart nor brain was engaged. An easy interception hit him in the chest. JB didn't understand why he never made an effort to catch the ball. It was the only time he could recall being yanked out of the game by a concerned Bear Bryant and left to finish his time on the bench in misery.

They lost. Badly. It was all his fault, he knew. The whole team left with their heads down. JB had his arm around Shelly, his latest flirt, one of the cheerleaders. He failed to see the slight figure standing alone at the gate, her fingers gripping the chain-link fence.

That night after his flight home, the nightmare returned. Clenching the sheets with wet hands, he was back in the middle of the battle, smothered by smoke and deafened by gunshots. Ellie was there, helping him, saving him.

She nursed him back to health. He knew he must have shouted her name.

Many of the girls told him he called out for an *Ellie* when he slept. It ruined more than a few relationships, he knew. Many a girl said it was hard to compete with a specter. He didn't know how they knew about the ghosts that haunted him, but they did. The dream possessed him, every friggin' night. It never concluded, never once, until that last day when he lost the game.

The dream started the way it usually did with a battle. This time JB heard the clear sound of a clock chiming loudly. JB rose from his sickbed, a homemade crutch under his shoulder.

"You have to leave." Ellie ran into the room. She was frantic, her face tense. She helped him into his uniform. "It's the Yankees. My father says they're on the way."

JB walked unevenly toward the door, dragging one leg behind him. Ellie clutched his shirt under his unbuttoned jacket.

She swung open the door, pushing him back as a blaze of torches lit the night sky. Slamming it shut, she turned to him. "You have to get out of here."

He fell against the wall, breathing heavily.

Ellie put her hand on the doorknob. "Go out the back way. I'll delay them," she said urgently.

"No." JB gripped her by both shoulders. I won't let you do that."

"Leave now, while you can. I'll be alright. We'll be alright."

"I don't want to leave you. I don't want to live without you."

"We'll always be together." She kissed him sweetly on the face. Her cheeks were wet with tears.

Ellie composed herself and opened the door, shouting to the strangers, "What do you want?"

JB stood there, frozen, unable to move. He heard a man's voice.

". . . know you're hiding . . ."

Ellie's strident denial was cut off by a gunshot.

"No!" JB dropped his crutch and swung open the door. Five shots went off at once, and he felt himself falling. He landed with a thud on the floorboards of the porch, his fingers linking with Ellie's limp ones before everything vanished. She looked at him, her eyes sad. Her mouth opened, and he heard her whisper, "I love you."

"No . . . ," he cried. "We need to finish this! We were supposed to be together!" His voice cracked as the world faded into gray mists.

JB sat up breathing as hard as if he had just run a race. Shelly tried to pull him back down, but he shook her off. He placed his hand on his chest, knowing that his heart had broken and would never be whole again.

9

TOUCHDOWN

It was freezing in New York in March. JB was totally unprepared for the weather. Back home, it could be downright sultry this time of year. He had to stop thinking of Alabama as home, though. He didn't know where his next home would be.

Today was the first day of the draft. They were on break now. Quarterbacks had been the first three picks.

The air was charged with excitement. Though JB was thrilled, there was a part of him that was dead as well. He existed by going through the motions, but his smiles never reached his eyes.

His friends all tried to set him up. The fit was never right. He knew he wasn't being fair, but didn't want anyone to feel the pain he lived with daily.

He was respectful, always letting the girls down gently. He knew he couldn't give more. There was nothing left.

He was sharing a smoke outside with some of the other players. They clustered around the hotel entrances, nervously laughing. He was smiling at something Roy Delacord said when sounds began to recede. He stood stock-still and sniffed. A pretzel truck gave off the aroma of roasting bread, but he knew he smelled something else. *He detected lilies.* The world crackled and shimmered. JB turned around in a slow circle, his keen eyes taking in every detail.

The tingling on his neck made his hair stand on end.

The busy New York streets were filled with brisk pedestrians. Lights changed, horns blared, and JB's insides trembled with the knowledge that something was going on.

Maybe the thrill of what was really happening had finally caught up with him, or perhaps it was something else. "Ellie," he whispered.

"What?" Roy asked, looking at him strangely. "Come on, Bud, we have to go in." Roy crushed his cigarette, and the two men walked inside. JB paused on the steps of the Belmont Hotel, searching the streets one more time before entering the building.

Green Bay. The Packers. If he thought New York was cold, wait until he played a game in Wisconsin. Coach Bryant slapped his back.

"You made it, son. I'm proud of you."

They both swiped their eyes, complaining that the tears must be from all that city pollution on the news they kept hearing about.

Coach Bryant pumped his hand and told him with no small amount of pride that he was one of the best players Alabama could ever have.

They all parted, some to celebrate and others to contact family.

JB couldn't wait to get out of the overheated ballroom. He left the building to stand on the sidewalk to see if he could sense that feeling again, catch the fragrance. He'd take anything.

He turned in a tight circle, the sun warming his face. Squinting, he looked at the four corners near the front of the building. He saw her.

She was standing by a light pole, watching the hotel intently. He saw her face register that he'd found her. She froze with horror and then took off, her heels making running difficult. JB sprinted after her. Her hat flew off, but he caught it without stopping, overtaking her in a New York minute and grabbing her by the elbow.

"Ellie!"

"No, let me go," she struggled.

A crowd cleared around them on the pavement. JB knew they were attracting attention.

A cop approached with his club out. "This man bothering you, Miss?"

They stopped struggling. Ellie's head was down. JB held out her hat, which she took from his hands. She shook her head. "No, Officer."

"Good." He nodded once and strolled away.

They stood together awkwardly, Ellie worrying the hat with tense fingers.

"Ellie!"

JB's heart was racing, words frozen in his throat. He didn't know where to begin.

"I've missed you."

Ellie nodded, but wouldn't meet his eyes.

"Where have you been all this time? I wrote you," he said in a rush.

Ellie shook her head and said with a humorless laugh, "Long story."

"What are you doing in New York?" JB blurted.

"I . . . I work here."

"Where?" JB looked around. "You're not in school?"

She glanced up, her blue eyes shiny with tears. JB took her hand, the touch sending sparks all the way to his bruised heart. He sensed she felt the same. She didn't pull away this time. "Let's go get a cup of coffee," he told her with a shaky voice. He felt rocked to his core. JB squinted at the sun but did not let go of her hand, afraid she would disappear like a ghost.

Ellie bit her lip with indecision.

"Don't you think we owe each other that?" he insisted.

She gave a curt nod and gestured toward a small storefront. "We can go there." They walked toward the coffee shop.

It was steaming hot inside.

JB helped Ellie out of her coat and then shrugged out of his. He had barely enough room to turn around. He filled the aisle so that patrons couldn't get around him when they wanted to leave.

He slid into a booth made for Keebler Elves.

Sitting opposite each other, they stared in pregnant silence. Ellie's eyes looked huge in her face.

JB could feel his knees touching the underside of the table, his shoulders squeezed into the small booth. He felt awkward and uncomfortable.

"You look different."

Ellie nodded, but her eyes were downcast.

JB cursed himself as an idiot and blurted, "In a good way. You look nice." He looked at her face. "You cut your hair."

Ellie's trembling hand touched the short cap of her curls. "Yes. It seemed appropriate."

Did she join a nunnery? "Appropriate for what?"

Ellie swallowed, then cleared her throat. "You, first."

"I wrote you a hundred letters. You . . . you only wrote once. You never responded to anything."

The waitress arrived with the coffee. He fumbled with the cup, which felt small in his hands.

"You're bigger than you were," she stated.

"I got drafted, today," he said with a tinge of pride. He knew his face had colored up. His ears burned.

"I know. I have been following your career. It was on the news."

"You listen to sports?"

She nodded, swallowing convulsively. In a low voice that he needed to lean forward to hear, she added, "Every day."

JB lit up with satisfaction and couldn't help the grin that appeared. He felt his face flush. He picked up his mug and it slid from his clumsy fingers, landing in the saucer with a loud clatter.

Ellie reached across the table and squeezed his hand reassuringly. Joy expanded in his chest and JB fought the urge to grab her and hug her right there and then. He smiled sheepishly and picked up the cup again.

He drank his coffee black. She toyed with the pink packets of fake sugar.

JB raised his hand and ordered two pieces of pie. The waitress brought them, carelessly sliding them across the Formica table. She tore off the check, giving them a dirty look before glancing behind at the line of people waiting for a table.

JB's big hand swallowed the bill. He slapped a twenty on the table.

Ellie looked up at him. "You're ready to leave?"

JB shook his head and said, "You didn't eat your pie." JB didn't want this time with her to end. He was afraid if he let her go he wouldn't see her again.

He looked down at the dry crust. "Not like home." He flicked off a pecan with his fork, popping it into his mouth. It was soft, but had a bitter taste as though it were burnt. He swallowed it and then pushed the plate away.

"So?" he said, his head cocked. He waited while she looked beyond him, as if she were looking for her history.

"I had to leave." A tear traveled down her cheek. JB studied her face. She was older, her face leaner. It had lost the youthful plumpness. Her eyes were serious, her expression sad, as if she carried some grave secret. He took a gulp of the now cold coffee.

"I had a baby."

JB spit out the coffee he had in his mouth. He coughed a few times, then wiped both his lips and tearing eyes.

"Are you married?" he gasped.

She shook her head. "No. His name is Josiah."

"That's my . . ." JB sat back, mute. His throat closed up as if he'd been strangled. "When?"

Ellie tapped the empty sugar packet on the table. "Oh, I don't know when exactly. Could have been that day in the truck or the other five times . . . It happened, and you went away. My parents were shamed. They sent me to a home for unwed mothers in Hartford."

JB's jaw worked. He said nothing. After a deep breath, he asked, "Did you know about it that day when I told you I made Bama?"

"Yes . . . no. I wasn't sure." She smiled slightly. "I was so mad at you. I suspected. That Scott woman had it all figured out, I think. She told my parents." She reached out impulsively to touch his hands. "I never saw your letters. My father must have destroyed them. I did try to contact you, but my parents prevented any mail from going out." Her face tightened.

"Where is he?"

She looked up, her eyebrows raised.

"My son," JB said it softly, then repeated it. "My son."

"In my apartment. Well, not now, really. He's in nursery school."

"Here, in New York?"

"Bayside. It's about thirty minutes away. In Queens."

"Why didn't you tell me?" He took her hands in his, cradling them.

"They wanted me to give him up." She looked away, swallowing again. He knew this was hard for her. "I wouldn't. They threw me out. I came here. My brother helped for a bit. I got a job, and we've lived here since. I went to see you once, in Pennsylvania. You were having a bad day. You lost the game."

He paused, recalling the day. "You were there?" JB's voice was barely audible. *He knew it!*

"I saw you leave with a girl. One of the cheerleaders. It was too much for me."

He squeezed her hand. His eyes were bright. "Let's go. I want to see him."

"I have to get back to work." Ellie smiled at him. She moved to slide out of the booth.

JB pulled her back. "Ellie, I never stopped loving you. I . . ." His voice was loud. All sounds in the diner quieted. People were looking at them.

Ellie hushed him, her thumbs making circling motions on his hands. It was strangely comforting.

"We'll talk later."

"Ellie, do you think you'll like Wisconsin?"

"Wisconsin?"

10

END ZONE

They had a good life. Married a few months later, once JB Junior got used to the idea of his new daddy.

None of their parents accepted the union, so they lived in new cities, wherever JB played. They moved first to Wisconsin and then to Texas a few years later.

JB had injuries, and Ellie nursed him. He was all thumbs when the girls came. He didn't know what to do with them.

Still, he missed home: the red Georgia soil, the lush greenery, the smell of ripe peaches.

Eventually, they bought a cabin there, which they used initially for vacations. Often, they went there when JB needed to recover, like after his concussions in '73, '78, and the last one in '81, which ended his career.

JB coached a bit, instead of using his engineering degree. He made a fair amount of money, and when his father died, he sold that damn peanut farm for millions of dollars.

Who knew the dirt was that valuable?

The kids grew up and went to different schools, met their own soul mates, and now JB could boast about his eight grandchildren.

JB's kids were spread out over the continental United States. Josiah, who answered only to Joe, and his wife lived in Sioux Falls. They settled there after his stint in the Air Force. Maureen and Monica resided in different cities in Florida.

JB and Ellie did get to see their daughters more. Monica's husband owned a restaurant near Disney, and Maureen's guy seemed to hop from job to job. JB liked him the least of all of his sons- and daughter-in-law.

But Monica loved him, and that was enough for JB.

He chose to keep his mouth shut, though. *Your life*, he told each one of his kids. *Who am I to tell you who to love? If it works for you, then it works for me*, he would say, and he patted both his girls' hands when he walked them down the aisle.

The end wasn't pretty for Ellie. It wasn't supposed to be that way.

It started with weakness in her hands. Then, her muscles began twitching, and she became unsteady on her feet, once falling badly enough to break her hip.

Ellie deteriorated, spending her final days on a ventilator.

It was bad, and JB buried her in the rear of the cabin. *Damn the ordinances.* It was his land, bought and overpaid for.

He'd been alone for the past few years, his sight failing a bit. He didn't tell the kids, of course. He missed her, his Ellie, and their life together. He had to admit, though, that they had certainly made up for lost time once they had finally gotten back together.

JB often thought about second chances, vagaries of fate, how *luck* or whatever one wants to call it placed them in each other's paths. He considered the detours of their lives, the misunderstandings that had driven them apart but brought them to joyful reunions that tasted sweeter than anything he could imagine.

They had had a good life. Busy, filled with happiness and the peace of knowing you got the *right* one, that life was for all the right reasons, and that you did well.

The nightmare had come back again recently. That ugly war resurfaced, bringing the horror of reliving another death, helpless to stop fate. Yes, sometimes, life wasn't fair, he knew, but the good times compensated for the bad.

The old clock chimed loudly filling the cabin with its crystal clear tones.

JB looked up, surprised. He realized that he had been dozing for hours. Must have overexerted himself with the rescue.

The clock rang again, with a musical quality. It made no sense; he hadn't wound it up, not for years.

It ticked loudly in the cottage, the comforting sound filling him with peace. It washed over him in waves, making his legs go limp and his body relax.

The air hummed with a peculiar energy and the back of his neck prickled. What was left of his hair stood up, and he smiled, knowing he looked like a mad scientist.

JB touched the area over his heart, feeling its rapid tattoo.

"Ellie?" he whispered. "Are you here?"

He felt the whisper of a hand caress his cheek.

JB closed his eyes with a sigh.

Her perfume surrounded him. *Lilies of the Valley.* He recognized it. She wore the same scent she had one hundred fifty years ago. *No, that was fifty years ago*, he corrected himself, his thoughts jumbling.

A cloud rolled into the room, and the air shimmered around him as if he were in a glittering ball. JB shivered when a warm lassitude enveloped him.

A form wavered in front of him. It danced like smoke from a flame and then took shape.

Cloudy at first, it solidified into Ellie, warm and beautiful, her eyes sparkling.

"I miss you," JB said simply. He meant it. He felt his heart thaw with longing.

He held out a hand toward her. Spotted and bent, it shook with age.

She reached for him, her skin supple and soft, young and whole.

He touched her, and a current ran through him, making his skin numb.

"Let's get you out of those old things," she said with a silvery laugh.

She tugged him up. When he rose, he saw his body slump like yesterday's laundry. He stood, tall and strong, young once more.

"I've missed you." He hugged her close, knowing he was back where he belonged.

Ellie rubbed her face on his chest, fitting against him like a long-lost puzzle piece or a key that had found its lock. "Well, I've been here waiting for you all along. Ready, JB?"

"I'll never let you go again."

They turned to the wall and stepped into eternity, connecting their souls once again forever.

AUTHOR'S NOTE

Thank you for reading JB and Ellie's story. I enjoyed sharing it with you.

While nobody in my fictional town of Bulwark is real, Bear Bryant did indeed exist. He was the head coach of the University of Alabama for twenty-five years. When he retired, he held the record for the most wins in history for a college football coach. He was known by his black and white houndstooth hat that was never far from his head.

My brother, Beta Reader, and friend helped me build Bear Bryant into the tapestry of the story, bringing both humanity and realism. His patience and fortitude are greatly appreciated. I could not have written JB's story without your wise counsel, Kevin.

My extended family, the ones here and the ones rooting from the ether, thank you for filling my life. My two brothers and their clans, you protected me when I was weak, you held out your hands so I wouldn't get lost. Thank you for being there when I needed you the most.

Writing is a combination of perspiration and inspiration. While the perspiration is all my own, the inspiration belongs to a big and diverse group of people.

RL Jackson is a bright and beautiful star who pushes our writing community to explore indie opportunities. Full of passion and fierce pride, she gets up time and time again when knocked down by adversity. She is the essence of indie.

Erica Graham, DJ Cooper, Brittney Leigh Bass, Kayleigh McLeod, Dell Henderson III, Katey Kelley, and RL, thank you for joining me in building the Bulwark Universe. Every character and each challenge of creating a new story prove the ingenuity of humanity and the incredible possibilities when people support each other and work together.

Brittney Leigh Bass serves double duty as a new author and my assistant. Thank you for furthering my dreams and making them a reality.

Beta Readers Shana Hurtes, Erin Glenn, and Julie A. Gerber keep the ball rolling and are an author's best friend.

Special thanks to my cheerleaders, Janey Glass, Stacey Chizzik, Erin Glenn, Alexis Wills, Marsha Hells, and, last but not least, Melinda "Molly" Casella. You don't know how much your faith and encouragement help.

My kids, Michael, Sharon, Eric, Jennifer, Alexander, Hallie, Cayla, and Zachary, you inspire and delight me every day. You dare me to be a better person, and I am blessed for each and every one of you. Is it trite to say you all complete me in so many different ways? Shall I stop gushing, kids? *Am I embarrassing you?* Sorry, but I have to say you are my proof that we have multiple soul mates, for I feel we are connected in an unbreakable chain that lasts forever. *What is a soul mate? Can we have more than one?* These are questions I've always considered. *Do we meet time and time again?* I'd like to think so.

Lastly, to my David, my heart, my bulwark. I feel you and know you are always there.

Brit Lunden
Hicksville, 2019

For more on my books or to get in touch with me–

Visit my website-
britlunden.com

Like my Facebook page-
facebook.com/britlunden

Follow me on Twitter-
twitter.com/BritLunden

Huge thanks to cover designer R.L. Jackson
authorrljackson.com

Read on for the first chapter from The Illusion, Volume Two of The Bulwark Anthology

The Illusion

DJ Cooper

1

CHAPTER ONE

"There's something I'd like to show you if you have a minute, Terence." Dr. Peter Kent shuffled his feet uncharacteristically as he addressed the junior police officer behind the station's desk. A phone rang at one end of the room and was answered on the third ring. Another conversation penetrated the awkward pause between the two men. Kent hesitated before continuing in a hushed tone, "I, I er, it's not a police matter. Maybe after your shift?" The young deputy's face reddened slightly. This dance of theirs had been progressing at a slow, torturous pace for months.

85

Terence nodded. "I finish at four today. Where shall I meet you?"

Dr. Kent felt a slight tightening in his chest and reached for the pen and notepad on the desk with hands shaking more than he'd like. "Text me when you're done. I know you might get caught up. I'll pick you up and drive us out there. It's not far."

Terence raised a single eyebrow in a questioning look. He already knew the phone number Kent had written on the paper. The deputy was intrigued. Bulwark had its moments, but things had quietened down in the last few weeks. Terence was up for a mystery that involved more than a stray dog and a garbage can. He nodded his consent and looked forward to his early finish on what could be a frantic Saturday.

Kent double tapped the desk with his knuckles. "Great, it's a date. I mean, I'll see you later and show it to you, my thing, I wanna… I mean… later." With wide eyes caused by the nonsense his mouth had just spewed forth, Dr. Peter Kent caught the glare of Sheriff Clay Finnes as he turned to leave. He wondered if the sheriff would ever get it through his thick skull how little threat the doctor posed to his interests, romantic or otherwise. Kent glanced back at the desk and saw the deputy shuffling papers. As the doctor turned to leave, Terence looked up and failed to make eye contact. That just about summed up what they may never get to call their relationship.

"What was that about?" Sheriff Finnes asked as he approached the desk.

The younger man's face flushed a second time as he contemplated his answer, "Oh he wants to show me something after work."

The sheriff grunted in response, "You be careful with him. He has a…" he paused and looked away into the distance, trying to find the word. "He has a reputation."

"Yeah, a false one," the deputy countered. He stopped short of reminding Finnes that he'd been sure the doctor was chasing Finnes' own wife not so long ago. It was a badly kept secret Terence was not supposed to know. It had taken the insistence of Jenna, Finnes' wife that she was definitely not the doctor's type. Yet still, the animosity remained.

"Just be careful with lover-boy," the sheriff said.

"He's not, I mean we're not, never mind." There didn't appear to be much Terence could do to persuade Sheriff Clay Finnes and others of two things, one that Terence wasn't a child and two that Dr. Peter Kent wasn't the devil.

Read the rest of the Bulwark Anthology!

Bulwark by Brit Lunden

The Knowing, Volume 1 by Brit Lunden

The Illusion, Volume 2 by DJ Cooper

The Craving, Volume 3 by R.L. Jackson

The Window, Volume 4 by E.H. Graham

The Missing Branch, Volume 5 by Kay MacLeod

The Body, Volume 6 by Kate Kelley

The Battle of Bulwark, Volume 7 by Del Henderson III

The Darkness, Volume 8 by Brittney Leigh

If you enjoyed this story, please leave a review on Amazon, Goodreads, or wherever else you love to talk about books. Thank you!